DC JOHNS
MEETS HIS
MATCH

An extract from the memoirs of
Detective Inspector Peter Johns

JUDY FORD

DC JOHNS MEETS HIS MATCH.

Published by Bernie Fazakerley Publications

This book is a work of fiction. Any references to real people, events, establishments, organisations or locales are intended only to provide sense of authenticity and are used fictitiously. All of the characters and events are entirely invented by the author. Any resemblances to persons living or dead are purely coincidental. No part of this book may be used, transmitted, stored or reproduced in any manner whatsoever without the author's written permission.

ISBN: 1-911083-15-5
ISBN-13: 978-1-911083-15-3

CONTENTS

1 MY FIRST MURDER

Looking back, 1975 was probably the most significant year of my life, with the most important events kicking off in the autumn, just after the annual 'Sunny Smiles' collection for the National Children's Home had finished. I'd been in CID for just on two years by then, but I hadn't been involved in anything as dramatic as a murder enquiry yet; so when DI Paige told me that we were going over to the nurses' home at the Radcliffe Infirmary to investigate a suspicious death, I was pretty excited. It was pure luck that I was in at the beginning: his favoured sergeant was on leave and I was the only DC on duty that night.

When we got there, we found a group of nurses sitting in their little kitchen with mugs of cocoa. There were four of them: Sister Catherine Spencer, Nurse Jane Bentham, Nurse Elaine Gregg and Nurse Angela Wheeler. They were all in their early twenties and all looking rather shell-shocked.

Sister Spencer was very much in charge. She was the one who had made the call to the police, after another of the nurses in their part of the home had been found dead in her bed that evening. She was a tall, dark-haired woman with deep brown eyes that watched intently as we entered the room. She rose to her feet and signalled to her colleagues to do the same, but Paige waved to them to stay seated. Although in some ways he could be old-fashioned in his outlook, Richard Paige had no sense of his own importance and did not stand on ceremony.

Nurse Bentham was shorter and fairer than Sister Spencer and less well turned-out. Both nurses had long hair secured in a bun at the nape of the neck but, while Sister Spencer's was neat and tidy, Nurse Bentham's had strands of mousey brown hair dangling from it and several hair grips protruding, as if ready to fall out at any minute. I noticed that nurse Bentham's mug of cocoa had left a brown ring on the kitchen table where it had spilled over while she was drinking it. She looked at us anxiously as if unsure what to expect.

Nurse Gregg was small, lively and garrulous – but perhaps that was just nerves in the presence of the police. She spoke rapidly in a strong Black Country accent, offering to make tea for us and repeating, over and over again, her opinion that it was incomprehensible that anyone should want to kill Susan Parry. As she talked, she took off her nurses' cap and I could see that her brown hair was cut so that the upper layers were shorter than those beneath, in a way that was fashionable at that time. She and Nurse Bentham were both wearing their nurses' uniforms, while the others were in civvies.

Lastly, we come to Nurse Wheeler, who stood out from the group because she was what we used to call at that time 'coloured', which is to say that she was of Afro-Caribbean origin. I later learned that she had come to Oxford from Jamaica only a few months earlier. Her hair was braided across her head in an intricate pattern, in a way that I had never seen before. Her eyes were bright and intelligent. She was of medium height with a curvaceous and beautifully proportioned figure.

Paige started by speaking to the group as a whole. We learned that Nurse Susan Parry had been found dead that evening, when some of her colleagues had gone into her room to investigate why she had not appeared on the ward for her night shift. Sister Spencer had called for help and a doctor had come over from the hospital and examined the body. He had concluded that she had been killed by a stab wound to her chest and had ordered the nurses to call the police.

At this point, Paige stopped the conversation and, after giving the nurses strict instructions to stay where they were, took me to inspect the body. A uniformed constable was guarding the entrance to the bedroom where the remains of Nurse Parry lay. He opened it for us and we went in and looked down at the shape beneath the sheet. Paige reached out and pulled down the covers to reveal a slim, blond figure wearing brushed cotton pyjamas, which lay open at the front, presumably unbuttoned by the doctor who had examined the body. Paige pointed silently at a narrow incision in her chest. A tiny trickle of blood had dried on her skin just below it and there was a small round stain on the sheet beneath. Then he covered up the body again with the sheet and looked round the room.

I followed his gaze, trying to work out what he might be looking for and what he was able to deduce from what he saw. Everything looked very ordinary to me; there was nothing obviously out of place. Paige prowled round, looking at the shelves and peering under the bed.

Suddenly he pounced on a key, which was lying on a small table next to the bed. He picked it up, using a handkerchief so as not to put his own fingerprints on it, and tried it in the door. It turned easily.

'Hmm!' he murmured. 'We seem to have a classic locked-room murder, with our victim inside, the key beside her and the murderer apparently vanished into thin air!'

He replaced the key on the bedside table and went over to the window, craning his neck to see down to the paved area outside, two floors below. Finally, he checked that the window was closed and the catch was fastened.

'Nothing obvious in here,' he said at last, 'but we'll get forensics to go over it in case our killer left any traces behind. Now we'd better get back to those nurses and put them out of their misery. If we take two each we can get their preliminary statements and then let them get off to bed. We'll have a better idea what we really need to know after we get the PM report.'

I started my interviews with Angela Wheeler. She sat at the kitchen table, very calm and business-like, brushing aside my apology for questioning her at such a difficult time. She told me that she occupied the room next to Nurse Parry's. This gave me an opening to ask when she had last seen the dead nurse.

'Very briefly at the handover on the ward this morning. We're both on male surgical. I'm on "earlies" this week, while she's on nights.'

'I see; and before that?'

'That would be yesterday afternoon. She always goes straight to bed after a night shift and generally gets up sometime in the middle of the afternoon. I met her as I was coming in after my shift. She was on her way out to do some shopping.'

'And over the last few days, did Nurse Parry seem just as normal? She wasn't anxious about anything, as far as you know?'

'Now you ask,' Angela answered, screwing up her face in a very endearing way, like a child with a hard sum to work out, 'she did seem a bit worried these last couple of weeks; but I thought it was just that she was anxious in case she made any mistakes with a patient. She's newly qualified and it is rather daunting for a new nurse to think that we're responsible for people's lives, especially at night, when there's often only one qualified nurse on duty; it's difficult to know sometimes whether a situation warrants getting the on-call doctor out of bed. Susan takes her responsibilities very seriously and I thought she was just nervous about having to make decisions on her own.'

'I see. Now, just for the record, can you describe your own movements from eleven last night to when Sister Spencer called us?'

'Let me see. Well, I was in bed before eleven last night. I got up at six, got dressed, had breakfast and went over to the ward in time for the start of my shift at seven. I was on the ward until half past three, when I came back over here and changed out of my uniform. I nipped out to the shops, then came back and had a cup of tea in the kitchen with Jill Saunders: she's the other nurse who shares this part of the home; you haven't met her because she's on nights. That would be about half past four.'

'Ah yes. Can I check that I've got it straight? There are six of you sharing this part of the home? And it has a door separating it from the other parts, with a lock that only the six of you have keys for?'

'Well, Mrs Fish, the housekeeper, has a master key and so do Security, but apart from that, yes, only the six of us can open the door.'

'And you each have keys to your own rooms? Do you all keep them locked?'

'When we're out and when we're in bed at night, but I don't think any of us bothers during the daytime if we're in.'

'But Nurse Parry's room was locked when you went to look for her just now: Sister Spencer said that she had to get the master key from the housekeeper's room.'

'Yes. I suppose Susan must have locked it so that no-one would disturb her while she was asleep.'

'The key wasn't in the lock. Do you know where she kept it?'

'She used to put it in her purse when she went out, but I don't know what she did if she locked the door when she was in her room.'

'OK. Now, you were, where, when Nurse Bentham came in looking for Nurse Parry?'

'I was in the passage on my way to the kitchen to make

myself some cocoa before bed.'

'And when you met Nurse Bentham you went with her to look for Nurse Parry?'

'Yes. I knocked on the door but there was no reply. Then Elaine and Catherine came up the stairs and Catherine went to telephone to see if Susan might have gone over to the ward after all.'

'And when she came back with the master key, who went in first?'

'Catherine. She opened the door and went in and we all followed her. We all saw that Susan was dead. Catherine checked her pulse and told us to go back and wait in the kitchen. She went down to telephone for help from the hall.'

'And did she lock the door, after you all left?'

'Yes. She said we'd better make sure that no-one wandered in and disturbed anything.'

'I see, so none of you were in the room alone at all?'

'No. We all went in together and came out again together.'

'And Sister Spencer was the first in and the last out?'

'Yes.'

And that was that for the time being. Angela went off to her room and I turned my attention to Nurse Bentham. She was only too eager to tell me everything that had happened that evening in the greatest of detail, interspersing her narrative with her own ideas on what steps the police ought to take in order to discover who had managed to get into her colleague's room and stab her to death as she slept. As I struggled to keep up with her narrative, I wished that I had made more effort to improve my shorthand speed and I was conscious of having to ask my witness to repeat things so that I could be sure that I had got her statements right in my notes. Eventually she ran out of steam and I sent her to her room, telling her to expect to be questioned again at some later date.

As soon as we had finished interviewing the nurses,

Paige insisted that we go round to Nurse Parry's home in Bicester to break the news to her parents, despite the lateness of the hour. It was a rule of his that, as the chief investigating officer in a murder case, he should always inform the victim's family himself personally and at the earliest opportunity. This is a rule that I tried to follow myself when I became sufficiently senior to be in charge. It's important for the family to know that they are being treated with respect and that they don't get to hear about their loss through the grapevine – or worse still through the news media – before being officially informed.

As was to be expected, Mr and Mrs Parry found it hard to take in the fact that their daughter had been murdered. They were unable to think of anyone who might have borne her a grudge and were not aware of any arguments or fallings-out between Susan and her flatmates. The only possible help that they could give to the investigation was a vague feeling, expressed by Mrs Parry, that Susan had been uneasy about something that had happened on the ward and had been worrying about whether or not to report it.

2 THE INVESTIGATION CONTINUES

The next day DI Paige called us all together and briefed his team on the incident.

'On the face of it,' he said, 'we have just five suspects: the other nurses who shared the flat in the nurses' home with Nurse Parry. They – and the housekeeper – are the only people with access to the flat.'

'But someone else could have got hold of a key,' Detective Sergeant Egerton pointed out; always keen to make his presence felt. 'They could have "borrowed" the housekeeper's key – or maybe one of the nurses got a spare key cut for a friend – or, well there are all sorts of ways of getting through a locked door, aren't there, sir?'

'Yes,' Paige conceded, 'that's true; and so we're going to be asking everyone with a legitimate copy of the key to check that it hasn't gone missing and to tell us all about where they keep them and whether anyone else could have got hold of it for long enough to make a copy.'

Egerton smiled complacently, obviously thinking that he had impressed Paige with his perspicacity, but I thought that the Inspector looked rather irritated by the interruption.

'However,' he continued, 'any outsider would be taking

a big risk of being noticed by one of the nurses on their way to Nurse Parry's room after they'd got into the flat. I think it's much more likely that our murderer is one of the resident nurses. And there's also the question of the locked room to consider. The murderer must have also had a key to Nurse Parry's room, since the door and window were both locked – and in any case, the room is on the second floor, so an exit through the window is out of the question. It's much more likely that our killer was an insider: one of the nurses who live in that flat. But, since you're so interested in the matter of keys, Egerton, you can take care of that side of the investigation. You need to find out what records are kept of keys to the nurses' quarters. Ask to see the names of everyone who's been given a key to that flat, going back for the last ten years – especially anyone who had a key to Nurse Parry's room as well. She'd only been living there for a few months, so it's possible that the previous occupant still has a copy of the key. Oh! And while you're about it, you might as well do the rounds of all the local key-cutting places to see if any of them remember cutting a key of the design of the flat and/or room keys.'

'Yes sir,' Egerton answered, sounding rather deflated. I guessed that he must have realised that Paige hadn't been impressed by his comment after all.

Paige despatched a team of officers to interview staff at the hospital, beginning with those who worked on the same ward as Susan Parry.

'Find out everything you can about her,' he instructed, 'particularly who her friends were and whether she'd fallen out with any of them recently. And find out if there have been any incidents reported on the ward or any complaints made about any of the nurses – especially about Parry or the others from her flat.'

Once everyone else had left to go about their assigned tasks, Paige turned to me.

'I want you to stay with me,' he said. 'We need to

interview the other nurse from the flat and compare what she says with what the others told us yesterday.'

'Yes sir.' I hesitated, unsure whether to voice what was on my mind in case it was presumptuous of me to make suggestions about the conduct of the case; but Paige detected the uncertainty in my voice and urged me to speak up.

'I was just thinking, sir, that it might be better to wait until the afternoon. She was on the night shift last night and will most likely be in bed now.'

'That's a very good point,' Paige said, encouragingly. 'So let's put off going back to the nurses' home until this afternoon. Meanwhile let's have a look at what we've got so far and then there's some work for you to do going through the files to see if any of our suspects has a police record – or if any of them reported any crime.'

We sat down together at Paige's desk. I felt very privileged to have been singled out to work with him and tried my best to create a good impression. I drew up a table showing where each of our suspects had been during the period when Nurse Parry could have been killed.

It looked as if Angela Wheeler was in the clear, because she had been on duty on the ward for the whole time, but we would have to check with the staff there whether she had left at any point and been absent for long enough to return to the nurses' home. Catherine Spencer had a daytime shift in the operating theatres, so she could have slipped in and stabbed Parry before leaving for work that morning. Jane Bentham and Elaine Gregg were both on the late shift that day, so either of them would have had plenty of time to kill their flatmate before going over to the hospital. Bentham worked on the same ward as Parry; so if there was any truth in Mrs Parry's assertion that her daughter was worried about something not right there, that might provide a motive. The fifth nurse – Jill Saunders – was supposedly asleep when Parry was killed, but she could have got up, done the deed and then gone back to bed.

My careful searching of the police records drew a blank. None of the nurses had any sort of criminal past and none seemed to have been the victim of crime either. The only hint of anything dubious was a caution for possession of cannabis issued five years previously to one Graham Lawson, who was now (according to the talkative Jane Bentham) sister Spencer's boyfriend.

3 NURSE WHEELER

Several weeks passed without any breakthrough in the case. It must have been very uncomfortable for the five remaining nurses in the dead girl's residential group. They were all aware that they were under suspicion and they all knew that one of them was almost certainly a murderer. I felt guilty every time we went back to question them further about their relationships with Susan Parry or to cross-examine their colleagues as to their characters and their movements.

Having been brought up by the National Children's Home, I always try to support their fund-raising events. So, when the annual Festival of Queens came around I went along to the Town Hall to watch the pageantry. I suppose I'd better explain what the festival was. Each year Sunday School children and Brownie packs used to raise money for the National Children's home by selling 'Sunny Smiles'. These were pictures of children who were being cared for by the Home. I don't think I was ever considered photogenic enough to be one of those depicted in the little booklets that were distributed all over the country. When all the money was in, the collectors used to come together for a show, at which each church and Brownie pack dressed up a little girl as a queen for the day.

I chose a seat near the back where it would be easy to get out if an urgent call were to come through from Paige. Just as the show was starting, who should come in and sit down next to me but Nurse Wheeler? She looked very attractive in what I took to be her Sunday best: a dark red dress beneath a black coat.

I hesitated before addressing her, thinking that the last thing she would want was to have to talk to someone from the police investigation team; but then I thought that it would be worse if she recognised me and thought that I was following her as part of a surveillance operation. So I spoke to her and I was very gratified that she remembered my name. She told me that she was there with the children from the Sunday School at her church. She'd helped with making the costumes for the queen and her two attendants. We watched the procession of queens walking up the aisle and I congratulated Angela on 'her' queen's costume. Then suddenly the conversation took a more sinister turn.

'It reminds me a bit,' Angela whispered, 'of carnival back home. Only there it's out of doors and rather less restrained.'

'Well, with the British weather, it's rather risky doing things out of doors,' I whispered back, just trying to make conversation. 'And with the British temperament, you would expect restraint!'

'So would you say that West Indians are very different from British people?' Angela asked sharply. It sounded as if I'd hit a nerve, although I couldn't think why.

'No – at least I don't know. I was just joking about the famous British reserve. What are you getting at?'

'A little while ago,' Angela said, speaking slowly and in an undertone, 'I overheard someone saying that West Indians were the sort of people who might very well stab someone to death while they were in bed asleep.'

'What!' I shouted out, unable to help myself. Then I

saw people turning to look at us and I forced myself to whisper again. I took Angie by the hand and insisted on going outside where we could talk properly. I wanted to know who had been saying such ridiculous things. Angie didn't want to tell me, but I insisted. I was afraid that she might think that I suspected her of killing her friend – or at least that I might be biased in that direction.

'It was just one of the nursing auxiliaries. I expect she didn't mean anything by it.'

'You don't imagine that the police have that attitude, do you? I mean, surely you must realise that you of all people are not under suspicion?'

'Because I was on the ward that morning? I thought there was a theory that I might have come back during my lunch break.'

I suddenly realised how much pressure our ongoing investigation must have been having on the nurses in Angie's group. I tried to reassure her, forgetting for a moment that I shouldn't be sharing information about the case with anyone outside of the police team.

'No. We had to consider that possibility, but it doesn't work. Look – I shouldn't be telling you this, so you must keep it absolutely to yourself, but the medical evidence shows that she had to have been killed before eleven that morning. And you were on the ward in sight of other staff until half past twelve. So you really are not a suspect.'

I waited for a while to let that sink in before going back to the question of who it was who had suggested that Angie was the murderer.

'Now, I really wish you'd tell me who it was that made that vile accusation against you.'

But Angie wouldn't say.

'No really,' she insisted, 'I couldn't. I'm sure she didn't mean anything by it. It wouldn't be fair for her to get into trouble over something that probably lots of other people were saying – or at any rate thinking – people who didn't get overheard.'

Of course, that only made me see red all the more. I don't know what she must have thought of me, ranting on the way I did.

'What do you mean "other people"? Has this sort of thing happened before?'

'Oh it's nothing,' Angie said dismissively, obviously trying to get me to shut up. 'It's only natural, I suppose, to be nervous of people who are different.'

'But you're not different – not underneath – not in the things that are important! What business have they got saying that you're different?'

'Please Peter,' Angie begged, 'stop worrying about it. It doesn't bother me. It's just one of those things. OK?'

I wasn't convinced, but I could see that Angie didn't want to take things any further. It made me angry that I couldn't go and have it out with the nursing auxiliary – and anyone else who had said similar things – but then I remembered how awkward I felt as a child when one of the teachers heard the other children bullying me over my ginger hair and told them off in front of the whole school. I guessed that Angie was afraid of me making a similar scene.

We decided not to go back to the show, and went for a walk in Christ Church Meadow instead. Angie told me about her family back in the West Indies; about how she was managing to save a little out of her nurse's salary to send back to them to help support a brother with cerebral palsy; and about how much she missed her parents and siblings. I became more and more impressed with her as she talked about her family life and her hopes for the future. All too soon, it was time for us to go back to the Town Hall so that she could escort her Sunday School children back home.

4 AN UNPLEASANT INCIDENT

The next day, I had another nasty experience of the casual racism that was all too common in those days. I was in the canteen having my lunch with a few of the other younger men. They were all very keen to talk about the upcoming dance and about whom they were planning to take with them. I didn't have anyone to take and was keeping quiet hoping that no-one would ask me about it but, of course, they were determined to know.

'What about you, Johns? Who're you taking?' one of them asked.

'I haven't decided yet.'

'Johns won't have any trouble finding someone,' another of them chipped in, 'what with him having been up at the nurses' home practically every day for the last few weeks. He must know lots of lovely young nurses who'd all be delighted to be asked.'

'I hear one of the ones he's been seeing is a coloured girl. I reckon she'd be a good bet. They can't get enough of it, I'm told.'

'Enough of what?' I asked stupidly.

'Poor Johns!' one of them mocked. 'He's led a very sheltered life. It comes of being raised in an orphanage I suppose.'

'What Constable Adams is saying,' another chipped in, 'Is that coloured girls are usually up for a bit of "how's your father" – especially with a white man.'

'How dare you!' Against my better judgement I flared up, which was, of course, the worst possible thing to do. 'You've no right making that sort of suggestion about someone you haven't even met.'

'Ooh! Hark at him. I reckon Johns is sweet on that coloured nurse!'

'Look at him! He didn't deny it. He fancies her!'

Well, I could hardly stay after that, so I left the rest of my lunch and walked out with as much dignity as I could muster. What I didn't realise was that Paige had been sitting at the next table and had heard everything. He brought up the subject that afternoon, while we were on our way to the hospital to interview the Theatre staff to get more background on Sister Spencer.

'It was brave of you to stand up to Adams and his cronies. I was at the next table. I heard it all. You were right to pull them up about assumptions about people on the basis of race. That's part of being a good policeman: never assume you know what a person's like just because of what they look like, or where they live or what job they do.'

I wasn't used to receiving compliments from senior officers and I didn't know quite how to react. In the end, I think I mumbled something about it not being a matter of bravery.

'I just didn't like what they were saying about Angela,' I explained.

'It's Angela now is it?'

And of course then I realised that I'd given away more than I intended about my feelings about Angie. Paige was obliged to remind me that she was still an important witness in a murder enquiry and any relationship with one of the police investigation team would be completely inappropriate. Then, to my surprise, he went on to say something that made it clear to me that he could read me like a book and had a complete grasp of the situation.

'However, once the enquiry is over,' he said, 'that would be another thing altogether.'

5 LIGHT DAWNS

The following week, we had a breakthrough in the case. We discovered that a former patient on the ward where Nurse Parry worked had put in a complaint, saying that he had been denied pain-relief following his operation. The incident had happened during the period when Sister Catherine Spencer was working there, and it turned out that she was the nurse who had signed for the diamorphine that the patient claimed he had never been given.

That set us off on the path of further investigation of Sister Spencer's private life and in particular her boyfriend, Graham Lawson. We discovered that he had progressed from cannabis to harder drugs and it did not take long to establish that Spencer had been supplying him with diamorphine from the hospital stock. From there, we soon found out that Susan Parry had become aware of an occasion when Spencer had signed for a dose of diamorphine and then 'forgotten' to give it to the patient; and after that everything started to fall into place. Within a matter of days, we had Catherine Spencer and her boyfriend under arrest and it wasn't long before we were in a position to charge her with the murder.

I was pleased that Paige took the trouble to go over to

the nurses' home before the news was released to the public, to tell Angela and the others that they were no longer under suspicion. He asked me to go with him, which seemed odd at the time, but I discovered afterwards that it was all part of his plan.

We waited for them in the housekeeper's office. Once they were all there, Paige stood up to address the group.

'I wanted to speak to all of you,' he said, looking round at their expectant faces, 'because I know how difficult it has been for you over the past few weeks, knowing that we have had to treat you as potential suspects in the murder of Susan Parry. I wanted you all to know that you are none of you any longer under any kind of suspicion, and I hope that we shall not need to question any of you again.'

He paused to let the news sink in.

'Please, Inspector,' Jill Saunders asked, 'does this mean that you know who killed Susan?'

'Yes Nurse Saunders, it does. I'm prepared to tell you who it is because the press will no doubt soon get hold of the information, but I'd like to emphasise that anything I say to you now is to be treated as strictly confidential. I'm sure that, as nurses, you understand what that means. Not a word of what is said here to anyone outside this room – and especially nothing to any newspaper reporters. Do you understand?'

They all nodded eagerly.

'Very well,' he continued, 'I can inform you that Sister Catherine Spencer has been charged with the murder of Nurse Susan Parry. I can also tell you – and this is where you must remember not to repeat what you've heard – that she has signed a confession, which makes it clear that she was acting alone. We are therefore not looking for anyone else in connection with this murder.'

There was a short silence while they all considered this news.

'But why did she do it?' Jane Bentham asked at last, voicing what they had all been thinking. 'What had she got against Susan?'

'Sister Spencer had been stealing diamorphine from the ward stock and she was afraid that Nurse Parry had discovered about it. She killed her to prevent her telling anyone.'

'So is Catherine Spencer a drug addict?' Jane asked in astonishment. 'She didn't behave like one. I'd never have guessed.'

'No. She wasn't stealing for herself. She took the drug to give to her boyfriend.'

'But how did she manage it?' Jill asked. 'Drugs like diamorphine are very carefully monitored. Someone would have noticed that it had gone missing.'

'But it was recorded as having been given to the patients,' Angie broke in. To my surprise, she had already worked out how Spencer had managed to keep her thefts secret for so long. 'She wrote up in the patient notes that she'd administered it, but she just pocketed the phial instead. That's why that patient complained that he hadn't been given any pain killers.'

'That's correct,' Paige agreed. 'She usually only played that trick once with each patient, but she made a mistake with that one and he was left without any pain relief for twelve hours following surgery. When he put in his complaint, it helped us to put two and two together.'

'So let me get this straight,' Elaine said slowly. 'Catherine was stealing diamorphine from the ward and Susan got wind of it and threatened to expose her?'

'I don't think it was a strong as that,' I intervened to stop them thinking that the dead nurse had been a blackmailer. 'As far as we can tell, she didn't make any threats. She thought that Sister Spencer had forgotten to administer the drug to one patient. She talked to her about it and they went and gave it to him. But she was thinking of reporting the incident as a 'near miss' because Spencer shouldn't have written up the notes until after she'd actually given the drug.'

'And Spencer was afraid that, if the incident was investigated, other instances when she'd purloined the drug instead of giving it to a patient might be found out,' Paige continued.

'So then, a few days later, she waited for Susan to come off her night duty and went in and stabbed her to death in her bed, before going on duty herself?' Elaine asked. It looked as if she must have been keeping her own notes and wanted to check what we said against them.

'That's right,' Paige confirmed. 'Working in Theatres, it was easy for her to take away a scalpel from the autoclave one evening and to return it to the hospital the following morning. Her nurse training enabled her to inflict a fatal wound to the heart – something which is not nearly as easy as most people think. She locked the door when she left, using Parry's key, which she replaced on the bedside table when she came in with the rest of you that evening. None of you noticed her putting it there, because you were all too busy looking at the body.'

He looked round at the four faces in front of him.

'Now, that's all I want to say to you. Remember what I said about not passing this on to anyone else. I'm sorry it has taken so long, but I hope that you can all now sleep easy again.'

They got up to go, but Paige called Angie back.

'Nurse Wheeler! If you wouldn't mind staying just for a couple of minutes, Constable Johns has one or two loose ends to tie up and he'd like to ask you some questions.'

He left the room, ushering the other nurses ahead of him. We were left alone. For a moment or two, I couldn't think what to say. Paige hadn't mentioned to me that he was going to do this. I wondered what he was expecting me to say to Angie.

'I wanted to ask you,' I began, still trying to think of something to say. Then I had an idea and tried again. 'There's a police dance next week. I was wondering if you might be willing to go with me.'

Angela looked surprised for a moment and then burst out laughing.

'Is that what the inspector meant when he said you had some questions for me?'

'I don't know, but that's the only question on my mind at the moment.'

'Oh Peter! Of course I'd love to come, but how did inspector Paige know you wanted to ask me?'

'Oh, nothing much gets past him.'

That's about the end of the story, but there was an incident at the dance that I probably ought to tell you about. It shows something of the sort of man Paige is and why it is that we always worked together so well after that.

6 THE POLICE BALL

Paige arrived in the company of a rather overweight and spotty WPC, whom I assumed he had asked out of pity because she couldn't find anyone else to take her. I didn't really want to allow Angela to dance with anyone apart from me: partly because I wanted her to myself, but also because I didn't trust some of my colleagues to treat her properly. Of course, when Richard Paige asked her for accompany him on the floor, I could hardly protest. She told me afterwards about the conversation she had with him as they tripped the light fantastic.

'Why did you want Peter to ask me to the dance?' she asked boldly. 'I mean that was the loose end that you said he needed to tie up wasn't it?'

'I didn't want to be stuck here all evening making conversation with WPC Jacobs,' Richard answered in a deadpan voice.

'If you didn't want her company, why did you invite her?' Angie enquired innocently.

'Because I didn't want to have to listen to her for months afterwards sighing and saying what a pity it was that she hadn't been able to come.'

'Wouldn't it have been more straightforward to tell

Peter that he had to invite WPC Jacobs?'

'No, because then I'd have had Johns going round with a long face, which would have been almost as bad as Pam Jacobs and her moaning. Besides, you'll be good for Peter Johns. He could do with a woman to look after him.'

'Do you mean at the dance or in life generally?'

'Oh generally: it's not good for a policeman to go home to an empty house after spending the day looking at mangled corpses and interviewing victims of assault.'

'What about you then? Peter told me that you were still a bachelor yourself.'

'But I live with my father and grandmother. Thirty-five and still never left home: what d'you think of that?'

'I think your father is a very lucky man.'

'What a very diplomatic answer. I thought you would probably think I was very unadventurous, considering you've travelled half way round the world to be here.'

'I had good reason for coming here. It sounds to me as if you had equally good reasons for staying at home.'

The music reached a conclusion and Richard brought Angie back to join me again. I was with WPC Jacobs, standing close to the bar where a cluster of young men had gathered to collect drinks to take back to their partners. One of them turned to go, lurched sideways and collided with Angie, spilling the contents of his glass down the front of her dress. I immediately recognised him as Adams, the ringleader of the group from the canteen. He was evidently rather drunk.

'Oh look Johns!' he called out, 'your monkey's spilled my drink.'

For a few moments there was a stunned silence in that part of the room. I could hardly believe my ears: surely even Adams must know that this was not the sort of language that he could expect to get away with here? Angie took a step back, looking down and brushing the lager from her dress with her hand to hide her confusion. Pam Jacobs put her arm round her and offered her a paper serviette, which she had picked up from the bar. I recovered enough to step forward with the intention of giving Adams what for, but Richard was too quick for me. He calmly placed himself between us and looked Adams squarely in the face.

'Peter,' he said, without turning his head. 'I think Miss Wheeler would like you to take her outside for a breath of air. The atmosphere in here has suddenly become very unpleasant.'

I knew better than to argue. I took Angela's arm and led her from the room. I found out afterwards that Richard gave Adams a proper dressing-down in front of everyone. I certainly wouldn't have liked to be in his shoes.

Angie and I went outside into the cool night air and stood on the steps of the hall. I wasn't sure what to do next. I was afraid that this experience might have put her off the idea of going out with a policeman.

'I think I'd like to go home now,' Angela said after a while.

'Yes, of course. I'll walk you back to the nurses' home.'

We set off, walking silently arm in arm.

'I don't suppose he meant any harm,' Angie said. 'I expect it was just the drink talking.'

I thought that it was nice of her to try to give Adams the benefit of the doubt, but I knew she was wrong. Anyway, I was in no mood to let him get away with anything. This incident reminded me too much of something that had happened years previously, and which had made a great impression on me.

'There were a couple of coloured girls in my house,' I told Angie, remembering the scene. 'Sisters. They were five and three when they came. One day, one of the boys made a monkey joke about them. We were all sitting round the table having our tea. I can still see it now. A lot of us laughed at it. Even one of the coloured girls joined in.'

I stopped to think for a minute. Angie didn't say anything, so I went on.

'I never saw my House Father so angry either before or since. He didn't raise his voice; he just spoke in a sort of calm fury. I must have been about ten at the time. I was terrified. He told the boy that his remark was the sort of thing that had sent millions of Jews to the gas chambers. He told the rest of us that anyone who laughed at the joke was just as bad as the boy who made it. He said that for evil to triumph all that is needed is for good people to stand by and do nothing.'

'I think it was a bit hard on a ten-year-old, comparing you to the Nazis.'

'But he was right. That's where that sort of thing starts. I made up my mind, then and there, never to be a party to making fun of someone because of their appearance – after all, I get enough of it myself because of my hair! Anyway, it wasn't being called a Nazi that struck home; it was feeling that he was disappointed in us. I bet that's how Adams is feeling now, with Richard Paige giving him a dressing down. Richard's very well respected in the force.'

'He must be young for an inspector,' Angie commented.

'Yes, but then he lives and breathes the police, so it's no wonder he's a high flyer. I shouldn't think he's ever had a girlfriend or any sort of social life.'

'Thirty-five isn't too old to start,' Angie said, but I could tell she was just teasing me, so I played along with it.

'Oh well, that's it then!' I declared, as if I were taking her seriously. 'If I'm in competition with old Richard I might as well give up now. Shall I go back and fetch him so that he can take you home?'

'Don't be silly, Peter,' Angie giggled, squeezing my arm. 'I much prefer redheads – didn't I tell you?'

THANK YOU

Thank you for taking the time to read DC Johns Meets his Match. If you enjoyed it, please consider telling your friends or posting a short review. Word of mouth is an author's best friend and much appreciated. Thank you,

Judy.

MORE ABOUT PETER AND HIS FRIENDS

Peter features in five more books.

- **Awayday**: a traditional detective story set among the dons of an Oxford college.
- **Changing Scenes of Life**: DCI Jonah Porter's life story, told through the medium of his favourite hymns.
- **Despise not your Mother**: the story of Bernie Fazakerley's quest to learn about her dead husband's past.
- **Two Little Dickie Birds**: a murder mystery for DI Peter Johns and his Sergeant, Paul Godwin.
- **Murder of a Martian**: a double murder for Peter and Jonah to solve.

Read more about Bernie Fazakerley and her friends and family at https://sites.google.com/site/llanwrdafamily/

Visit the Bernie Fazakerley Publications Facebook page here:
https://www.facebook.com/Bernie.Fazakerley.Publications

Follow Bernie on Twitter: https://twitter.com/BernieFaz.

ABOUT THE AUTHOR

Like her main character, Bernie Fazakerley, Judy Ford is an Oxford graduate and a mathematician. Unlike Bernie, Judy grew up in a middle-class family in the South London stockbroker belt. After moving to the North West and working in Liverpool, Judy fell in love with the Scouse people and created Bernie to reflect their unique qualities.

As a Methodist Local Preacher, Judy often tells her congregation, "I see my role as asking the questions and leaving you to think out your own answers." She carries this philosophy forward into her writing and she hopes that readers will find themselves challenged to think as well as being entertained.